MICHAEL DAHL PRESENTS

MIDNIGHT LIBRARY 4D

The Lost Lenore

by Thomas Kingsley Troupe

illustrated by Xavier Bonet

STONE ARCH BOOKS
a capstone imprint

Michael Dahl Presents is published by Stone Arch Books,
A Capstone Imprint
1710 Roe Crest Drive
North Mankato, Minnesota 56003
www.mycapstone.com

Library of Congress Cataloging-in-Publication Data is
available on the Library of Congress website.

Summary:
Cobblestone floors, heavy, dusty books, quills and
parchment—the library has transformed. The clues: strange
rustling sounds, a gentle rapping, and a black feather or
two. Who's to blame? It's Poe's Raven, of course, come to
find the lost Lenore. But Lenore only exists in the poem . . .
doesn't she?

ISBN: 978-1-4965-7893-8 (hardcover)
ISBN: 978-1-4965-7897-6 (eBook PDF)

Printed and bound in the USA
PA48

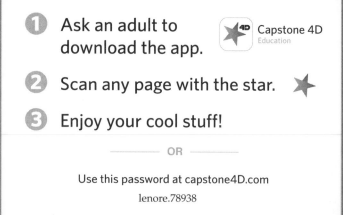

1 Ask an adult to
download the app.

Capstone 4D
Education

2 Scan any page with the star.

3 Enjoy your cool stuff!

——— OR ———

Use this password at capstone4D.com

lenore.78938

MICHAEL
DAHL
PRESENTS

Michael Dahl has written about werewolves, magicians, and superheroes. He loves funny books, scary books, and mysterious books. Every Michael Dahl Presents book is chosen by Michael himself and written by an author he loves. The books are about favorite subjects like monster aliens, haunted houses, farting pigs, or magical powers that go haywire. Read on!

Midnight Library

The **MIDNIGHT LIBRARY** was named after T. Middleton Nightingale, or "Mid Night." More than 100 years ago, Nightingale built the library but then vanished. The giant clock in the library went silent. Its hands froze at twelve. Since that day, no one has heard the clock chime again. Except for the librarian Javier and his team of young Pages. Whenever they hear it strike twelve, the library transforms. The world inside a book becomes real—along with its dangers. Whether it's mysteries to be solved or threats to be defeated, it's up to the librarian and his Pages to return the Midnight Library to normal.

The Librarian
JAVIER O'LEARY — Javier is supervisor of the library's Page program.

The Pages

BARU REDDY — He reads a lot of horror books. And his memory is awesome.

JORDAN YOUNG — Her parents have banned video games for the summer. She hopes working at the library might get her access to gaming on the library computers.

KELLY GENDELMAN — She figures helping at the library will be fun. Maybe the other Pages will appreciate her love of bad puns.

CAL PETERSON — His parents think the library is a good place to expose him to more books. They never expected him to go *inside* a book!

CHAPTER ONE
Distant Toll

Cal Peterson moved his finger along the library shelf until he found the right spot. He wedged the World War II book—*Codes and Codebreakers*—into the gap. He sighed and turned back to his book cart, selecting another book. *Why couldn't people just put the books back in the right spot?* Cal had been shelving for what felt like hours, and he had barely made a dent.

He couldn't stop thinking about the old, broken clock Javier had shown him and the other volunteer Pages on their first day. It was in the middle of the massive library. Both of the clock's hands were stuck at twelve.

"You'll hear the gong of midnight and you'll see," Javier had said. "But don't be scared. You're not losing your mind. You're just inside an *author's* mind. The five of us will be able to work together to make things right."

Cal was pulled out of the thought by Kelly's voice. She stood beside him with three books under her arm. She didn't seem to be in any sort of rush to get through her cart of books to reshelve.

"You think it's going to happen again?" Kelly asked nervously. "The thing with the clock?"

Cal turned to look at her. "I don't know," he said. "I hope not. But I also hope it does, if that makes sense."

Kelly nodded and looked at her phone. "It should happen in a few minutes, if it does."

Before Cal could reply, Rolene, the information desk librarian, walked over, frowning. She was wearing glasses and had her hair piled on top of her head. She carried at least nine books in her arms, stacked up to her chin. She stopped at Kelly's cart.

The woman mumbled something. Cal thought it sounded like, "Good morning." She dropped her books onto Kelly's cart.

"I need to get back downstairs to my desk," Rolene said with a tired voice. "Would you put these tomes back in their home?"

Cal watched Kelly hold back a sigh. "Sure," she said. "No problem."

"It seems like there's a ton of work to do here at the library," Cal said. "Is there any reason there aren't more of us helping out?"

"A ton of work is right. Not that anyone cares if I'm dead tired by the end of each day. But you four were chosen!" Rolene said. "And there can only be four. Never less, never more." The woman walked away, mumbling under her breath.

"Huh. She's interesting," Kelly said.

"Yeah," Cal replied. "Really interesting. She called the books 'tomes.'"

Before they could say more, there was a distant sound: the gong of a bell. It sounded muffled, as if it tolled from far away, but each strike made the shelves and books vibrate.

One, two.

Cal watched the ladder in the aisle shake and roll a bit along the carpet.

Three, four.

Cal pulled out his phone and checked the time. It was 12:00 p.m. *Right on time,* he thought.

Five, six.

With each gong, the entire library transformed before his eyes. The books changed from crisp and colorful new hardcovers to old, dusty-looking volumes.

Seven, eight.

The carpeted floor turned into cobblestones. The dim electric lights became lanterns with flickering candles inside of them.

Nine, ten.

A hazy fog circled their feet.

Eleven.

Cal sniffed the air. It smelled like fire and old leather.

Twelve.

"Well, this is new," Kelly said. She reached out and touched the old books lined up on their black shelves. "I mean, old, actually."

"Here we go," Cal muttered.

Things were about to get interesting.

CHAPTER TWO

The Bucket Man

Cal glanced around the library. A cold,
damp breeze blew through an open window
in one stone wall. Its purple curtains billowed
in the wind, like old ghosts. Outside the moon
glowed over a misty graveyard. A leafless tree,
swaying in the wind, looked like a skeletal
hand bursting out of the ground.

"Baru? Jordan?" Cal called.

"They can't hear us," Kelly said. Then she shouted, "Javier! Are you here?"

"I'm here!" someone shouted. Footsteps pounded toward them. It was Javier.

"Thank goodness," Cal said. "This place is—"

"Beyond creepy," Javier said. "I know. But try not to worry about it."

"The whole place just turned dark and spooky," Kelly said. "I don't know how to not worry about it!"

Suddenly a black streak flew past them. Cal whipped around and saw it. Perched on the corner of a tall shelf was a shadowy figure. It had shiny, dark eyes and a long, sharp beak.

"It's a raven," Cal said, pointing. "An enormous one."

The raven cawed. It wasn't afraid of them.

The bird didn't move. Which at least meant it didn't come any closer. And Cal didn't have time to worry much more about it, because just then, he saw Baru and Jordan running toward them.

"Oh, good," Javier said. "You're all here. Let's get to work."

"Last time we helped teach a spider named Charlotte how to spell," Cal said. "And that brought us back where we belonged. Anybody know where we are now?"

"This is right up my alley, unlike the world of E. B. White and *Charlotte's Web*," Baru said. He was the horror fan of the group. "But

I don't know whose work this is yet. It'll come to me."

"Hopefully soon," Cal said. "I don't like the look of this place."

Jordan crossed her arms and tossed her hair. "I don't like it either," she said. "And my dad would NOT be happy to see where his little girl is right now."

The rest of the group ignored that.

"Does the raven mean anything to any of you?" Javier asked.

"No," Cal said, looking up at the enormous bird. It was staring straight at him. "But it looks like it wants something, doesn't it?"

"It probably wants to get out of here as much as we do," Kelly said.

CAW! said the raven.

Then they heard a deep, hoarse voice. "WHERE . . . IS SHE . . . ?"

Cal looked around, but no one was there. A cold breeze filled the room. He heard footsteps. They sounded like they were coming closer to him with each step.

"Over here," Javier whispered. He pointed to one of the large wooden tables. The five of them crowded together underneath.

A hulking figure holding a large bucket stepped from the shadows. Slop dripped from the end of the trowel he held in his other hand. The sight of the slop made Cal shudder.

"Gross," Jordan whispered.

The man paused, looked down an aisle, and

then turned. "WHERE . . . IS . . . SHE?" the man moaned as he thumped away.

"That was weird," Kelly said.

"Super weird," Cal agreed. He stuck his head out and looked down the aisle. "Come on. It looks like he's gone."

They climbed out from beneath the table. The raven still sat atop a bookshelf, staring down at them.

"OK, what's with the bird?" Jordan asked. "It looks like it wants to eat us."

"I'm not sure," Javier said. "I haven't seen it before. I don't think it could eat us, though. Peck our eyes out, maybe, but—"

The raven crowed and then tapped and rapped at the bookshelf a few times. Then it flapped its large wings and adjusted its claws on the shelf, gazing down at them.

"OK," Jordan said. "Not helping."

They watched as the raven spread its wings and glided onto a sculpture of a woman's head a few yards away. The bird squawked and pecked the stony surface a few times. Then it looked at them again, as if waiting for something.

"Whose head is that?" Baru asked.

Javier walked over and squinted at the carving. "I'm not sure," he said. "I've never seen this sculpture before."

"Um, hello?" Jordan called. "Can we focus here? We've got a mean-looking bird and an even meaner-looking bucket man on the loose in here."

"That's Pallas," Kelly said. "The Goddess of Wisdom." The other kids stared at her, and she shrugged. "I had to do a project on Greek mythology for school," she said.

Baru clapped. "That's it! I know who the bird is!"

"Wait," Cal said. "What do you mean? And keep it down. I don't want Bucket Man to come back here."

Baru turned to the raven, still watching them from its perch atop Pallas. "Greetings, bird," Baru said. "Do you have anything to say to us?"

Cal laughed. "Seriously, Baru? Birds can't talk."

"Nevermore," squawked the raven.

CHAPTER THREE
Rapping, Tapping

The Pages and Javier stood around the raven in awe.

"Aha!" Baru said. "I was right."

"Explain," Jordan said. "Please."

"It's from Edgar Allan Poe's poem 'The Raven,'" Baru said proudly. "I read it a while back, along with some of his scary stories. In the poem, the raven perches right on top of this head!"

"But it talks," Jordan whispered. "That bird just said—"

"Nevermore," the raven said again, cutting her off.

"So we're stuck . . . where?" Cal asked.

"In Edgar Allan Poe's world," Baru said. "At least, I think so."

"I've never read anything by Poe," Kelly said. "But I get the feeling he was a little strange."

The raven tapped and rapped its beak against the statue head. It cocked its head as though it were waiting, and then croaked, "Nevermore!"

"Can that bird say anything else?" Cal asked.

"No," Baru said. "And it's what drove the narrator in Poe's poem mad. It seemed like the bird wanted to tell him something, but 'nevermore' was all it could say."

"Got it," Cal said. "We should get out of here before it drives us mad too."

"Javier, has the library ever changed to Poe's version before?" Jordan asked.

"No," Javier said. "It's different each time. And each time I've felt like I was in some sort of dream. Like the worlds in these stories and poems are released from their pages and made real for a short time."

CAW! The raven rapped against the stone head again.

"He doesn't like being ignored," Jordan said.

"Does anyone?" Kelly asked. "The Poe thing."

Jordan narrowed her eyes, but didn't respond. "Maybe he's hungry," she said. "Anyone got some bread or something?"

"No," Baru said. "But that wouldn't work anyway. Ravens usually eat carrion. You know, rotting meat or roadkill. So unless anyone has any of that . . ."

"Gross. Forget it," Jordan said.

"Nevermore," the raven squawked, and then tapped again.

"I got it!" Cal yelled. "Does anyone have a piece of paper?"

Javier reached into his back pocket and produced what looked like a folded piece of ancient parchment, inked with a fancy script.

"This was my grocery list," Javier said, eyeing the paper. "It seems to have . . . changed."

Cal flipped the paper over to the blank side and found a spot at a table. "Anyone have a pen?" he asked.

Jordan pointed at the table, and Cal turned. There was a feather quill stuck in an inkwell a few inches away.

"Oh," Cal said. "Right."

"What are you doing?" Kelly asked. She sat down next to him.

"I think that raven is trying to say more

than his favorite word," Cal said. "But I might be wrong."

He dipped the end of the quill into the ink. Then he waited. After a moment, the raven tapped and rapped his beak against the statue. When the bird tapped, Cal made marks on the paper. Quick taps were recorded with a single dot. Longer, harder taps he captured with a dash.

This went on for a little while, and then the bird stopped.

"Oh, wow," Javier said, peering over Cal's shoulder. "That looks like—"

"Morse code," Cal said. He held up the paper and smiled. "That bird is trying to tell us something!"

CHAPTER FOUR

Undead Red

"Wait a second," Kelly said. "Wasn't Edgar Allan Poe from like . . . a long time ago? Was Morse code even invented then?"

Cal hadn't thought of that.

"Too bad the books have all changed," Baru said, gesturing around the library. "We could look it up."

Javier shook his head. "Actually, the contents of the books are the same. They just have a *Poe*-etic look to them in this version of the world." He chuckled.

"I remember some of the letters," Cal said. "You know, S-O-S. But not all of them. If we can find a book with the Morse code alphabet, that'd help."

"To the three-eighties!" Javier cried, thrusting his fist into the air. "Come on. Follow me."

They stood up. But before they could head upstairs to the nonfiction section, a horrifying figure emerged from the darkened doorway. It was tall and had the face of a long-dead corpse. It wore tattered clothes, streaked with red, that looked as if they'd been rotting for years. It stared at the group with dark, empty eyes.

"Um . . . everyone?" Kelly whispered. "You're all seeing this too, right?"

As if in response, the creature raised a rotten hand toward them.

"*Bring . . . her to . . . me,*" the figure ordered. The monster's voice came out in a ragged hiss, as though its throat were damaged. Or rotting away. Which, Cal thought, it probably was.

"I hope he's not talking about me," Jordan cried, backing away.

Slowly, the tattered corpse took another step in their direction. The raven crowed and tapped the stone head again.

Cal felt his heart thunder in his chest.

Despite his fear, he snatched up the piece of paper and quill he'd used to record the raven's Morse code.

Tap-tap-tap-tap.

"We have to decode the tapping," said Cal.

Baru took a deep breath. "No time. I know what that thing is," he whispered, fear on his face. "And we need to run. Now!"

Cal and the others didn't need to be told twice. The entire group turned and ran toward the staircase, darting across the common area of the library.

"This way," Javier said. "Come on."

He led them upstairs to a dimly lit aisle. "Cal, you and Baru come with me," Javier said. "We'll find the Morse code books. Kelly and Jordan, wait here, where you can see downstairs and be our lookouts. Keep an eye on the . . . well, whatever it is. If it moves, hurry over to the three-eighties and find us."

"Wait!" said Jordan, stopping them. "What is that thing? It looks like a zombie. And I can smell it from here."

"It's the Red Death," Baru said quietly. "It's another character from Poe's work, I'm afraid."

"We've got company," Kelly said. She pointed across the room. It was the man with the bucket, walking into the stacks.

"They both seem to be looking for someone," Cal said.

"That's right," Jordan said. "That dude with the bucket said '*Where is she?*'"

"And the Red Death zombie thing said *'Bring her to me,'*" Cal said. "Was that in any of those books, Baru?"

Baru was quiet for a moment. Cal imagined he was trying to sift through his vast memory bank of horror stories.

"I don't remember the Red Death looking for a woman," Baru said. "That thing was more of a symbol for a nasty disease that was spreading."

"A real disease?" Kelly asked.

"No, no," Baru said. "It was something Poe made up, but in his story, it wiped out everyone at a masquerade party."

"Everyone?" said Jordan quietly.

"So in this world, the plague could be real," Kelly said. "Great."

"Exactly," Baru said. "Which is why I think it's best we stay away from that thing."

The library was quiet for a moment. In the distance, Cal heard the distinct raps and taps of the raven.

It's a message, Cal thought. *I just know it!*

"Show us where the three-eighties are," Cal said to Javier. "The raven has some sort of message for us."

Jordan shivered. "Hurry up," she said. "I don't like being split up for long."

As the boys followed Javier winding his way through the stacks, Baru turned to Cal. "Jordan's right, you know," said Baru. "In horror movies the bad stuff always happens when the heroes split up."

CHAPTER FIVE

Books and Mortar

Cal and Baru followed Javier across the second floor, deep into the nonfiction stacks. But before they reached the 380s, where the Morse code books were shelved, Javier stopped short.

"Shhh," he whispered, putting a finger to his lips.

Cal and Baru followed Javier's gaze.

The Bucket Man had changed locations. He was just a few feet ahead, with his back toward them.

Cal, Baru, and Javier watched as the man dipped his trowel into the bucket and spread what looked like wet cement onto the back of a thick book. Very carefully, he set the book onto another book, also dripping with cement.

He's building a wall . . . of books? Cal couldn't understand. *Why?*

"This is not good," Baru said.

"What's he doing?" Cal asked.

"In many of Edgar Allan Poe's stories, horrible things happen," Baru explained.

"One thing Poe was obsessed with? Being buried alive."

"He often wrote about people who were trapped somewhere unsafe or hiding dead bodies in strange places," added Javier.

"Oh no," Cal said. "What story is this guy from?"

"I think 'The Black Cat,'" Baru said. "In it, the narrator accidentally kills his wife and tries to hide her body in the wall. He seals it up with bricks. And since the Bucket Man doesn't have any bricks . . ."

"He's using books," Cal murmured. "Perfect."

"I don't see a dead body," Javier said. "Unless . . . You think he's going to put one of *us* in there?"

"We have to stay away from him," Cal said suddenly. "Let's not give him any ideas."

Javier sighed. "There's only one problem," he whispered. "We can't get to the Morse code book." He pointed to a shelf a few feet past the man with the bucket. "I can even see where the book is. I'll just try to sneak by him and get it."

"No way," Cal said. "It'd be easier for one of us to go and grab it."

Javier thought about it. "OK," he said. "But please, be careful. If he starts to turn, run back here as fast as you can."

"You got it," Cal said. "Which book is it?"

Javier pointed toward the shelf. Cal could

make out a dark blue volume. It seemed to have been bound in leather . . . or some other kind of skin.

"That one. See it? The blue one," Javier said.

Cal nodded. "Be right back," he said.

Cal crouched down and walked slowly toward the shelf. The Bucket Man grunted and sighed as he built his wall.

After what seemed like a heart-pounding eternity, Cal reached the bookshelf. None of the books had titles printed on the spine, but he knew the blue book was the one he needed. He reached out and touched the spine.

But as he did, he heard a sharp whisper.

"Not that one!"

Cal whipped around. Javier was shaking his head and motioning with his hands to the left. Cal tried another book, but Javier kept shaking his head.

"The *blue* one!" Javier whispered.

"They're *all* blue!" Cal whispered back.

But he was too loud. The Bucket Man turned. He stared at them with his bloodshot, angry eyes.

"YOU!" he growled. "YOU KNOW WHERE SHE IS!"

Cal was pretty sure his heart was going to break every rib in his chest from beating so hard. He grabbed three blue books, then turned to run.

But the Bucket Man blocked his way.

"Cal!" shouted Baru.

Cal stood frozen. The Bucket Man's slobbery lips parted to reveal a full set of fangs.

"Toss me that book," Baru whispered to Javier.

The librarian pulled down a heavy tome from the nearby shelf. "This one?" he asked. "But why do you want to read *Cannibal Legends of the South Seas*?"

"I don't want to read it," said Baru, grabbing the book.

"Get away from me, you lunk!" cried Cal to the huge man.

Baru hefted the book in his right hand.

Then he swung back and threw the tome directly at the Bucket Man's wall of books.

CRAAASH!

The books, covered in the wet, drippy cement, collapsed. The Bucket Man roared in anger. He lurched toward the falling books. Cal ducked under the man's arms, almost slipped on the wet cement, and ran back to Javier and Baru. The three of them headed toward the center of the second floor, where Jordan and Kelly were waiting.

As soon as they emerged from the stacks, Jordan and Kelly joined them and they all ran downstairs, taking the steps two at a time. Behind them, heavy footsteps thundered against the flat stone stairs. The big guy was chasing them.

"I hope that book is worth it, Cal," Jordan said. "Because that dude is *not* happy with us!"

"I'm not even sure I got the right book," Cal called back to her.

Downstairs, Javier led them toward the administrative offices—or what were the offices in the actual library. Cal was relieved to see there were rooms there, and that the rooms had doors, and that the doors had locks.

They ran inside the first one and slammed the door. In the darkness, they were almost afraid to breathe.

CHAPTER SIX

Rapid Research

"Does anyone have a candle?" Cal whispered. He wasn't sure anyone would hear him over the beating of his tell-tale heart. "I need to look at the books."

"There's a monster after us and you still want to figure out what that bird is saying?" Jordan asked.

Cal could hear a drawer open, and then the strike of a match. "Here," Javier said, lighting a long, thin candle and passing it over.

"How'd you know that was there?" Kelly asked.

Javier smiled. In the candlelight, his face—all of their faces—looked creepy. "The emergency supplies are stored in that drawer. Of course in *our* library, that's an AED and a flashlight."

"Well, it works for me," Cal said. He held the candle above the books and sighed with relief. "Yes, this one I grabbed is the right one!"

"Cal was right," said Baru. "All those books *are* blue."

"The Morse code book is blue," Javier pointed out. "The other ones are indigo and teal."

Cal paged through until he found a diagram showing the letters that corresponded with each Morse code. Then he compared it to the marks he'd made on the parchment.

"HELP ME," Cal read aloud. He looked up at the rest of the group. "The raven is saying '*help me.*'"

Kelly shuddered. "That bird is creepy," she said. "Do you think we *should* help it?"

"Can I look?" Baru asked.

Cal handed the book over. Baru flipped through it.

"This is interesting," Baru said. "Edgar

Allan Poe wrote 'The Raven' in 1845. And
Samuel Morse invented Morse code in 1836."

"So Poe could've known Morse code,
right?" Cal asked.

"For sure," Baru replied.

"OK, but what does any of this have to do
with the raven and what he needs help with?"
Kelly asked.

Just at that moment, they heard a rustle
of feathers outside the door. The raven was
perched outside. It tapped and rapped its beak
against the wooden door.

Cal grabbed the book away from Baru and
turned back to the code.

The raven pecked out more code.

Tap-tap-tap-tap.

When the raven was silent, Cal looked up. "FIND LENORE," he said. "What's a Lenore?"

Baru laughed and nodded in excitement. "Of course!" he said. "The poet's lost Lenore!"

"You're gonna have to explain that one," Cal said.

"I've never read much Poe," Javier admitted. "Too creepy. Except for that one about the pirate treasure and the gold bug."

"Well," Baru said, "Poe wrote his poem 'The Raven' about a guy who is looking for Lenore, his lost love. The guy's all messed up about it and the raven comes and blurts 'nevermore,' no matter what he says."

"So did Lenore . . . die?" Cal asked.

"Probably murdered by a bucket man," Jordan muttered.

Baru shrugged. "Hard to say," he said. "That's the thing about poems—you're sort of left to figure it out on your own."

"So maybe Lenore died and maybe she didn't," Kelly said. "That's kind of spooky."

"Totally," Cal said. "OK. So . . . what? The poet sent this bird out to find his lost girlfriend? Here? In the library?"

"That's gotta be it!" Baru said.

"You think she's here?" Javier asked. "Wow."

"Maybe those two creepy creatures are looking for her too!" Jordan cried.

"It's worth a shot," Kelly said, shrugging. She stood up. "Come on. Let's find Lenore."

"Seriously?" Jordan asked. "Did you forget about the Red Death and the bucket man?"

"I think Kelly's right," Baru said. "Lenore must be here somewhere. And we have no choice but to find her. Unless you want to stay here forever and never get the library to change back to normal?"

Jordan sighed. "Fine," she said. "Let's go. But this time we're sticking together."

Javier slid the heavy door open, and they walked back into the main room of the library.

Outside, the raven was waiting for them. As soon as all five people left the office, it hopped up and began to slowly fly away.

"Should we follow it?" Cal asked, looking at his friends. He put the Morse code book under his arm.

"Why not?" Javier said.

As the raven flew away, they followed close behind. It seemed to be heading toward the front of the library, where the main entrance was.

"Lenore?" Kelly called tentatively. "Are you here somewhere?"

The others joined in.

"Lenore!" Baru called.

"Hey, Lenore!" said Cal.

"Come on already, Lenore," Jordan said. "I want to get out of here!"

The raven stopped, landing gracefully on a table near the front entrance. It pointed its beak toward the door, and the five humans looked in that direction.

A woman sat behind an old, ornate desk, exactly where the information desk would be in the library back in the real world.

She was reading a book.

She seemed to be glowing.

She looked extremely familiar.

"Rolene?" Cal asked.

CHAPTER SEVEN
Just Mist

It was Rolene—the Nightingale Library's reference librarian. Sort of. This woman had long hair, all piled up on top of her head. Her face was smooth and flawless, as if spun from silk. She wore an old-fashioned gray dress.

Rolene was reading aloud. "'For the moon

never beams, without bringing me dreams, of the beautiful Annabel Lee.'" She sighed and looked up from her book. "Oh, hello," she whispered, smiling.

"That can't be Rolene," Javier said, shaking his head. "She wouldn't be here."

Cal took a step closer. "Rolene . . ."

"Wait a minute," Kelly said. "Lenore!"

"Rolene," Jordan corrected her. "Pay attention."

"No," Kelly said. "Lenore is an anagram for Rolene!"

Cal rearranged the letters in his mind. "You're right!" he said.

Kelly smiled at the woman. "You're Lenore, right?" she asked.

The woman smiled kindly in return, but instead of answering, she just held a finger to her lips. "Shhh!" she whispered.

"The raven wanted us to find you, Lenore," Cal said. "I think your poet guy misses you."

Lenore turned and looked up at the dark bird.

"He's been missing you for one hundred and seventy-three years," Baru said.

"That's some good math, book guy," Jordan said.

Lenore took a deep breath and sighed. With a look of complete calm, she placed a thin ribbon along the binding to keep her place and closed her book.

"I had to leave long ago," Lenore said. "I sought a place where I wasn't simply a dead woman in a sad poem."

"So you didn't really die?" Cal asked.

"In Poe's mind, yes," Lenore said. "He created me and just as quickly decided I could no longer live. The poem isn't the same if I'm still alive."

"Maybe he made a mistake," Jordan said. "Baru showed me the poem. It sounds like the guy in the poem wishes you'd come back."

"My dear," Lenore said. "This is where I belong, here among my first loves—books."

"Sure. If she went back, it changes everything," Cal said. "The poem doesn't work anymore if he's happy to see her again."

"You're right," Baru replied. He scratched the thick crop of dark hair on his head. "Poe's works were pretty dark. A burst of happiness like Lenore returning could completely upset his writing."

"So, Lenore isn't really *lost*," Kelly said. "It's just that she doesn't want to be found."

"Then she stays here," Cal said. "Simple. If Poe wrote that Lenore is lost, then that's how it should be. The narrator in the poem just needs to know that."

"So what's the plan?" Jordan asked. "Tell the bird to buzz off?"

"Not exactly," Cal said. He handed the Morse code book to Baru. Then he leaned over to the nearby table and picked up the feather quill that sat there. "We send a message and let him know that Lenore is happy where she is."

"But what's that going to do?" Jordan asked.

"I don't know," Cal admitted. "I've never written a message to a made-up guy in a poem before."

Before he could write anything, Kelly gripped his arm. "Look, Cal," she whispered.

Cal looked up, and a cold wave of terror washed over him. The Red Death had appeared in front of the information desk. The undead fiend reached out and grasped Lenore by the arm.

"You're . . . coming with me . . . ," it rasped.

The Pages and Javier scrambled backward in terror as Lenore struggled to free herself from the monster's grip.

"No!" Lenore shouted. "I belong here!"

"We have to do something," Kelly cried. "We can't let that thing take her!"

Jordan snatched the Morse code book away from Baru and flung it at the Red Death's face. The book struck dead meat, and the monster groaned. It instantly evaporated into a red mist. Its rotten, tattered clothes dropped to the ground.

"Nice shot!" Javier shouted.

Cal realized that was the second time that night someone had used a book to defeat evil.

Freed from the monster's grip, Lenore scrambled closer to the Pages. But a moment later, the red mist swirled and began to re-form into the monster. Slowly, it rose from the ground as if awakening from a long nap.

The raven cawed and rapidly tapped the edge of the shelf behind the desk.

Things are going to keep coming back to take Lenore if this poet doesn't stop looking for her, Cal thought.

The monster was quickly becoming solid again. Cal scribbled a note as fast as he could.

DEAR SIR,

WE'VE FOUND YOUR LOST LENORE. SHE'S HAPPY

WHERE SHE IS. PLEASE STOP BOTHERING HER.

THANK YOU.

SIGNED,

THE NIGHTINGALE LIBRARY PAGES

"That's harsh, Cal," Kelly said.

"The guy needs to take a hint," Cal said with a shrug.

With an eye on the approaching red zombie, he rolled the little message up into a scroll. He walked toward the raven and cringed when the monster bird cawed and flapped its wings once. Carefully, he extended the parchment to the bird.

"Bring this back to the poet, would you?" Cal asked.

As if it completely understood, the raven grasped the note in its claw.

"Here comes old Red!" Jordan shouted. "We have to do something, guys!"

"Go on," Kelly said. "Bring him the message, birdy."

The raven squatted, flapped its wings, and leapt into the air, circling the information desk once.

"Remind him to leave Lenore alone!" Cal shouted.

The bird circled faster and faster. The papers swirled from the wind created by the massive bird's wings.

"When does she want to hear from him again?" yelled Cal.

"NEVERMORE!" the raven cawed.

"Smart raven," Jordan said. "That's right!"

The Pages, Javier, and Lenore watched as the bird rose over the shelves. It flew through the doorway and was gone.

But the battle wasn't over.

They heard a groan. When Cal turned, he saw the Bucket Man lumbering toward them. An old guy dressed in pajamas approached from the other side. He had one giant eyeball.

Another man in a jester costume and clown make-up was galloping toward them from behind.

Poe's creations were coming from

everywhere. In seconds, they would be surrounded.

"I'm not sure it worked," Baru said.

The clock gonged once.

The entire library seemed to glow, and then it went dark.

Out of the shadows, an airy voice whispered, "Thank you . . . evermore."

Epilogue

As if in a blink, the T. Middleton Nightingale City Library was restored to its former glory. The darkness was lifted, and Poe's monsters were gone.

It worked, Cal thought. *He got the message.*

When the library was back to normal, Cal looked around. They all stood next to

Rolene's information desk at the front of the library.

Rolene was peering at them, one eyebrow raised. "Is everything OK?" she asked. "Mr. McLeary?"

"Just fine," Javier said. "How are you?"

"Oddly enough, I feel as if a weight has been lifted from my shoulders," Rolene said. "I'm not sure how to explain it." The woman stood up and gave them a radiant smile. She turned to the main doors. "Oh, look!" she cried. "The sun is shining, and the sky is bright blue. What a beautiful day! I think I'll take the rest of the day off. Is that OK with you, Mr. McLeary?"

Javier couldn't help but smile in return. "Yes, yes, of course," he said. "I'm just happy you're feeling better. C'mon, everyone. We should get back to work."

The others headed back to their book carts and reshelving. But Cal waited. He ran over to Rolene as she was pushing open the front doors, squinting at the bright sunlight.

"Your name isn't really Rolene, is it?" he said.

Rolene smiled again. Then she held her finger to her mouth. "Shhh," she said.

* * *

After he finished his book cart, Cal caught up with the rest of the group at a table in the common area.

Javier stood at the head of the table, looking a little worried. "So, that was a bit more . . .

interesting than I was expecting," he said. "I know you all understand the library and its . . . changes, but I can understand if you want to end your participation in the Page Program after today."

Cal looked around at the other Pages. But something caught his eye, and he turned. A small, golden bug that resembled a beetle skittered up one of the book carts. He wasn't sure, but it looked like there was a skull pattern on the bug's back.

"No way," Cal said. "I'll be here next Saturday. I mean, who knows what's going to happen next?"

INSIDE THE MIDNIGHT MIND OF . . . Edgar Allan Poe

When the Midnight clock chimes, the library transforms. Javier says each of these transformations takes the library "inside the mind of a book or writer." In this adventure, the Pages enter the mind of Edgar Allan Poe, the master of horror. Here are few of the bits floating around in that batty and bloodcurdling brain!

The Raven

The spooky bird comes from Poe's famous poem, "The Raven." Poe admitted he was inspired by a chatty raven named Grip from Charles Dickens' book *Barnaby Rudge*. Grip was based on Dickens' own pet. When the bird died, Dickens had him stuffed. Grip can now be seen in the Free Library in Philadelphia.

The Bucket Man

The Bucket Man builds a wall of books and mortar, blocking the way to the Morse code book. In Poe's tale, "The Black Cat," a man bricks up his dead wife and cat in a wall of his cellar. With a mixture of "mortar, sand, and hair," he glues the bricks together. The police discover the crime when they hear "a wailing shriek" behind the wall. Does it come from the dead woman or the mysterious cat?

Lenore

The narrator in Poe's poem, "The Raven," cannot stop thinking about his dead girlfriend, Lenore. Poe had written a poem thirteen years earlier called simply "Lenore" (I guess he liked that name) and she's dead in that poem too. In fact, there is a line that goes "weep now or never more!"

Michael Dahl

Glossary

anagram (AN-uh-gram)—a word or phrase made by rearranging the letters in another word or phrase

bloodshot (BLUHD-shaht)—eyes that are red and irritated

diagram (DYE-uh-gram)—a drawing or plan that explains something with the use of arrows, colors, shapes, and other things

eternity (i-TUR-ni-tee)—a seemingly endless amount of time

fiend (feend)—an evil person

jester (JES-tur)—a professional joker in medieval courts

masquerade (mas-kuh-RADE)—a party at which all the people dress up in costumes

Morse code (mors kode)—a communication system that uses light or sound in patterns of dots and dashes to represent letters and numbers

mythology (mi-THAH-luh-jee)—a group of myths, especially ones that belong to a particular culture or religion

participation (pahr-tis-uh-PAY-shuhn)—the act of joining with others to do something

tome (tome)—a large book

Discussion Questions

1. Edgar Allan Poe's world in the Midnight Library is one of the more dangerous places the Pages have had to visit. Which of the troubles they faced do you think was the most threatening?

2. In Poe's story, the Red Death is an illness, but in the Midnight Library, it's a physical monster. Why do you think they're different?

3. Rolene feels better in the real world after the Pages help Lenore. How do you think Lenore and Rolene are connected?

Writing Prompts

1. The raven communicates with Cal and the group through Morse code. Look up a Morse code alphabet and try to write some words down, such as your name or a short sentence.

2. Imagine the narrator of the poem still wants to see Lenore. Put yourself in the narrator's shoes and write a letter back to Cal explaining your feelings.

3. Edgar Allan Poe was famous for writing poems. Pick a character or monster from the story and write a poem from their perspective.

about the author

Thomas Kingsley Troupe has been making up stories ever since he was in short pants. As an "adult" he's the author of a whole lot of books for kids. When he's not writing, he enjoys movies, biking, taking naps, and hunting ghosts as a member of the Twin Cities Paranormal Society. Raised in "Nordeast" Minneapolis, he now lives in Woodbury, Minnesota, with his awe-inspiring family.

about the illustrator

Xavier Bonet is an illustrator and comic book artist who lives in Barcelona, Spain, with his wife and two children. He loves all retro stuff, video games, scary stories, and Mediterranean food, and cannot spend one hour without a pencil in his hand.